DUDLEY PUBLIC LIBRARIES

The loan of this book may be renewed if not required by other readers, by contacting the library from which it was borrowed.

1 7 FEB 2017

CP/494

D0193222

DUDLEY PUBLIC LIBRARIES	
000000913237	
£4.99	JF
25-Sep-2014	PETERS
JFP	

THE QUEEN'S TOKEN

PAMELA OLDFIELD

ILLUSTRATED BY JAMES DE LA RUE

BLOOMSBURY

LONDON NEW DELHI NEW YORK SYDNEY

White Wolves Series Consultant: Sue Ellis,
Centre for Literacy in Primary Education

This book can be used in the White Wolves Guided Reading
programme with children who need a lot of support with reading at
Year 4 level.

First published 2008 by
A & C Black
An imprint of Bloomsbury Publishing Plc
50 Bedford Square
London WC1B 3DP

www.bloomsbury.com

Text copyright © 2008 Pamela Oldfield
Illustrations copyright © 2008 James De La Rue

The rights of Pamela Oldfield and James De La Rue to
be identified as author and illustrator of this work respectively
have been asserted by them in accordance with the
Copyrights, Designs and Patents Act 1988.

ISBN 978-0-7136-8850-4

A CIP catalogue for this book is available from the British Library.

All rights reserved. No part of this publication may be
reproduced in any form or by any means – graphic, electronic
or mechanical, including photocopying, recording, taping
or information storage and retrieval systems – without
the prior permission in writing of the publishers.

This book is produced using paper that is made from wood grown
in managed, sustainable forests. It is natural, renewable and
recyclable. The logging and manufacturing processes conform
to the environmental regulations of the country of origin.

5 7 9 10 8 6 4

Printed and bound by CPI Group (UK) Ltd, Croydon, CR0 4YY

contents

Chapter One
A Gift From Millicent

Cheerfully, Hal Dibden swallowed his last crust of bread and few crumbs of cheese.

"You can't beat a bit of cheese," he told the cat. "Very tasty!"

The cat meowed hopefully.

"Go catch a mouse!" said Hal. "We've got nothing to spare."

He glanced at his grandfather, who had fallen into a doze.

Five years earlier, Hal's parents had died, and he now lived with the old man.

Granfer worked as a gardener for a rich family near the New Forest. Hal often helped him because he was strong, and could push the wooden wheelbarrow.

Sometimes, Hal worked in the stables, raking out the dirty straw.

Or he would exercise Dandy,
the pony who belonged to
Millicent, the rich man's daughter.
Then she would reward him with
a few small coins.

Suddenly, Granfer opened
his eyes. "You still here, lad?"
he demanded. "Get over to the
stables and earn your keep!"

He spoke roughly, but Hal
knew the old man loved him.

"I'm just going, Granfer," he
grinned, and set off at a run.

Millicent was about to be married to a wealthy man. Hal found her waiting outside the stables.

"I've a gift for you," she told him. "My husband-to-be wants me to ride a more elegant animal. Dandy is yours, if you want him, also the saddle and bridle."

Hal couldn't believe it. A pony of his own! As he stammered his thanks, Millicent hurried away, her long skirt held up to avoid the muddy cobbles underfoot.

"Some gift!" said Tommy, the stable lad. "The old nag could collapse any day."

Hal grinned. "I don't care. I shall ride the long way home tonight, so everyone will see us. Granfer is in for a big surprise!"

Tommy fetched some horse
blankets and shook them. "How
is your grandfather?"

"Still gardening,"
Hal said proudly.
"Granfer will work
until he drops!"

"And when he
does, you'll be
homeless," said Tommy.

Hal had often thought about
that. When Granfer died, a new
gardener would move into their
house. But Hal had a plan that
he'd been dreaming about for
many years.

13

"I shall go to London," he told Tommy. "I shall work as a gardener in King Henry's palace at Whitehall."

Tommy laughed. "Work for King Henry? You're mad!"

"Why shouldn't I?" asked Hal.
"I already know about trees,
shrubs and flowers, and I can
learn more."

Tommy lowered his voice. "You
watch your step, young Hal. The
king's a powerful, rich man, but
they say he has a terrible temper."

Hal laughed. "But I'd work
hard. King Henry would never
be angry with me."

Chapter Two
Dandy Disappears

When Hal finished his work, he saddled up Dandy and set off for home. He felt rather grand riding his own pony.

As he passed a woman washing clothes in the river, he pretended he was king and gave her a gracious wave. The woman hooted with laughter and waved back.

Hal rode on. They moved slowly because Dandy was hungry. Grass and wild flowers were plentiful, and the old pony nibbled everything in sight.

Thoughts of King Henry filled Hal's mind. He knew the king of England was handsome, could make music and enjoyed hunting, but they also said he ate too much and was becoming fat.

"He's a good king," Hal said aloud. "And his wife Catherine is a good queen. She comes from Spain, but can speak English now, and everyone loves her."

Dandy pricked up his ears at the sound of Hal's voice.

Hal grinned. "I thought you'd agree with me, Dandy!"

Granfer stared in astonishment as Hal rode up. He was amazed to hear what had happened.

"Well, bless my buttons!"
he said, scratching his head.
"That's a bit of luck for you, lad."

Hal went to bed that night
with a big smile on his face. He
was no longer just Hal Dibden –
he was the owner of a pony.

A week later, Hal was riding in the forest, dreaming of his exciting future. He didn't hear the music and laughter that was coming from somewhere among the trees. And he didn't see the rabbit that popped up in front of them and startled Dandy.

Suddenly, the old pony stopped in his tracks, and poor Hal lost his balance. As he fell from the saddle, Dandy galloped off into the greenwood.

Hal sat up, rubbed his head and counted his arms and legs.

"I'm still in one piece." He scrambled to his feet. "Now where is that silly animal!"

Hal called out again and again, but there was no sign of Dandy anywhere. He set off in search of the pony, but had only taken a few steps into the trees when he was grabbed from behind.

"What have we here?"
demanded a gruff voice.

Hal was lifted up and shaken
until his teeth ached. Turning
his head with difficulty, Hal saw
that his captor was dressed in
the uniform of the king's guard.
He began to panic.

"Stop wriggling, boy," the guard said gruffly. "I'm taking you to see the king!"

chapter Three
Hal in Danger

"Let me go!" cried Hal. "I'm looking for my pony, who has run away."

"A likely story." The guard glared at Hal with fierce, dark eyes. "I reckon you were spying on the king!"

"No, you're wrong! I'm not a spy!" Hal was puzzled. How could he be spying on the king? Surely the king was miles away, in his palace in London.

Then, for the first time, he noticed the sound of music and laughter. The New Forest was usually a peaceful place, where pigs and horses could roam at will. What on earth was happening?

The guard scowled. "King Henry is enjoying a picnic with Queen Catherine and their lords and ladies. You've been spying on them!"

"I haven't," Hal insisted.
"You must believe me. I have
to find my pony!"

Holding him by the arm,
the guard led Hal deeper into
the forest. Hal remembered what
Tommy had told him about King
Henry's temper, and began to
feel very afraid.

Suddenly, they came to a clearing. Fallen tree trunks covered with furs had been arranged around the grassy space, and elegantly dressed men and women were sitting on them. Hal had never seen so many silks and

velvets. The lords and ladies were being entertained by an acrobat, who was turning cartwheels, while another man walked around on stilts. A group of musicians played lively music, and a table was set with all kinds of wonderful food.

King Henry and Queen
Catherine sat in the middle of
their lords and ladies. The king
was smiling and clapping his
hands, and Hal began to feel
more hopeful.

The guard threw Hal on the
ground in front of the king.

"I've caught a spy, Your Majesty," he announced. "Sent by your enemies, no doubt."

The music ended abruptly, the acrobat stopped his cartwheels, and the man fell off his stilts. Everyone stared at Hal.

"I'm *not* a spy!" Hal cried into the dreadful silence.

King Henry stood up, put his hands on his hips and glared. "So *you* say!"

"I'm a stable boy." Hal's throat was so dry, his voice was no more than a croak.

One of the men bellowed,
"He's lying, Your
Grace!"

Another said,
"He looks like a spy
to me, Your Majesty."

"Send him to the Tower!"
cried one of the ladies, and all her
friends nodded in
agreement.

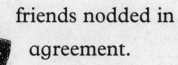

Soon everyone
began to suggest
horrible punishments.

"Throw him into the deepest
dungeon!"

"Chop off his head!"

Hal was terrified. Tommy had spoken the truth. King Henry was a *very* dangerous man – or so it seemed…

chapter Four
A Narrow Escape

Queen Catherine held out her
hand towards her husband.
"My sweet lord," she said gently.
"I beg you, stop this game.
You've all had
your fun, but
the poor boy is
frightened half
to death! He is
so very young,
I cannot think he is a spy."

She turned to Hal with a kindly smile, and he gave a little nod in return. Her elegant, green velvet gown and headdress sparkled with precious stones, and Catherine looked every inch a queen.

Hal was so grateful that he thought her the most wonderful woman in the world. But would the king grant his wife's request?

He held his breath.

Suddenly, the king began to laugh, and everyone joined in, cheering and clapping.

Hal felt weak with relief. It had all been a cruel joke. His trembling grew less, and his heart stopped thumping inside his chest.

King Henry sat down again. "If you are not a spy, then what are you? Tell us truly, and you shall be given a chicken drumstick from the royal table!"

So Hal told him about Granfer and the gardening, and how he had come by his pony

The king tossed him a chicken leg, which Hal just managed to catch.

Then, greatly daring, Hal told the king about his dream.

King Henry was all smiles now. "Then we shall find work for you in the royal gardens when you need it," he promised.

Hal stammered his thanks, and King Henry turned back to his friends.

The queen beckoned Hal closer. "The king may have forgotten you by that time," she whispered, "so I will give you a token of our good faith."

To Hal's surprise, the queen tugged a velvet-covered button

from the cuff of her gown and
pressed it into his hand. "When
you arrive at the palace, show
this button to the guards and tell
them it is my token. Say they are
to bring you to me post-haste.
I shall remember you, Hal."

Two years passed, and Hal grew
taller and stronger. He helped his
grandfather, and learned as much
as he could about seeds
and soil and plants.

One morning, when the cold
winter was giving way to spring,
Hal woke to find that Granfer had
died during the night.

Three days later, the old man was buried in the nearby churchyard. Hal walked home, his eyes full of tears, for he had loved his grandfather very much. Now he was all alone in the world.

"It's time to go to London," he said aloud. "Time to follow my dream." He spoke bravely, but he felt sad inside, and was fearful of the long journey ahead.

When he arrived home, he found a man and woman unloading a rickety cart. Two small children ran about, exploring. Hal's belongings were in a bundle by the roadside.

The new gardener had arrived.

Hal put on Dandy's saddle and bridle. "You can have the cat," he told the new gardener. "He's good at catching mice."

Then, without another word, Hal turned his back on his home, and set off for London.

chapter Five
The Queen's Token

That night, Hal slept under the
stars, huddled in his blanket.

The last thing he did before he went to sleep was to check the sleeve of his shirt. He had hidden Queen Catherine's button inside, where no one would see it. He must never lose the queen's token.

His journey to London took weeks, and Hal was often very tired and almost starving.

Hal trudged on. But now he had no money, no food, and no pony. He would have to beg for food and water.

"Will I ever reach the king's palace?" he wondered.

His dream was fading fast.

The next day, however, he
came across an old man sitting
under a hedge, looking very
dejected.

"I was on my way to London,"
he told Hal, "but I fell from the
back of a hay cart and hurt my
leg."

Hal cheered up at once.

"We'll go on together," he said. "Put your arm round my shoulder and I'll help you."

The man, who was a wandering storyteller, smiled gratefully as he struggled to his feet. "I'll tell you lots of stories to help pass the time," he promised.

They could only move slowly,
but after many weeks the two
friends reached London. They
wished each other well, shook
hands, and parted company.

Weary but triumphant, Hal
made his way to the king's palace.
He stumbled up to the gates, and
asked to see King Henry.

"The king has promised
me work in his garden," he said,
proudly.

The guard
laughed rudely
and said, "Get
away from here.
The king doesn't
see ragamuffins!"

When Hal tried to argue, the
guard lost his temper. "Argue with
the king's guard, would you?"

He grabbed hold of Hal and
dragged him into the palace,
where the king was sitting with
his ministers.

King Henry was not in a
good mood. "Work in the gardens?
I know of no such promise," he
snapped. "Give the boy a good
beating and throw him out."

Hal's heart was thumping with
fear, but he held out the beautiful,
velvet button.

"Your Majesty, this button was given to me by the queen. She gave it to me as a token of good faith. She told me to show it to you and ask to speak with her."

The king hesitated, clearly shocked. He took the button and studied it carefully. "Find Queen Catherine," he told the guard. "Take the button with you."

Hal waited, weak and anxious. Things were not looking good.

But when the queen arrived, she was smiling cheerfully. "How you have grown, Hal!" she cried.

Gently, she reminded the king about the meeting in the forest two years earlier. "This is Hal Dibden, the young spy!" she laughed.

"Remember how we teased the poor lad? Then you promised him work in the royal gardens. The button from my cuff was our token."

At last the king's frown was replaced by a broad smile.

"Then I shall certainly keep that promise," he told the queen, then he turned to Hal. "Tell the head gardener to set you to work, and find room for you in the royal stables."

Hal breathed a sigh of relief. Somehow, he had survived the journey. The worst was over.

Later that night, Hal climbed wearily onto the straw in the big room above the stables, which he shared with two other young gardeners and three stable boys.

After many long and weary weeks, his dream had finally come true.

"Thanks to the queen's token!" he whispered.

Tomorrow he would start his new life.

About the Author

Pamela Oldfield has written many books for young people of all ages – some funny, some serious. She particularly enjoys writing about history, and had fun learning about the Tudor kings and queens for *The Queen's Token*.

Pamela also writes stories for adults, mostly about the people who lived a long time ago and the exciting things that happened to them. She is always 'dreaming up' new stories.

Other White Wolves
historical stories...

WAR GAMES

James Riordan

It's Christmas Eve, 1914, and
there's a war on. British and German
soldiers sit in the muddy trenches
either side of No Man's Land, as
deadly enemies. Suddenly, a strange
sound fills the air. A German voice
is singing 'Silent Night'. A British
sergeant joins in, and so begins a
most unusual series of events...

War Games is a historical story set
during World War I.

ISBN: 9 780 7136 8750 7   £4.99

Other White Wolves
historical stories...

Outbreak

Alison Prince

Miriam doesn't understand why her
mum is buying more food than they
need, and storing it away. Or why her
parents have given her the nickname,
Mandy. Her friend Pam says it's
because war is coming. And, if the
Nazis invade, it will be dangerous for
her to have a Jewish name. But that's
not going to happen... Is it?

Outbreak is a historical story set
at the start of World War II.

ISBN: 9 780 7136 8840 5   £4.99

Year 4